A Doctor for the Animals

Introduction

Welcome to Half and Half books, a great combination of story and facts! You might want to read this book on your own. However, the section with real facts is a little more difficult to read than the story. You might find it helpful to read the facts section with your parent, or someone else, who can help you with the more difficult words. Your parent may also be able to answer any questions you have about the facts—or at least help you find more information!

A Doctor for the Animals

English Edition Copyright © 2008 by Treasure Bay, Inc.
English Edition translated by Nancy Doherty and edited by Sindy McKay
and Editorial Services of Los Angeles

Original Edition Copyright © 2004 by Nathan/VUEF, Paris – France
Original Edition: Le métier de vétérinaire

Julie's New Pet by Gérard Moncomble, Illustrated by Natali Fortier

Non-fiction text by Sidonie Van den Dries, Illustrated by Claire Brenier

Activity by Madeline Deny, photography by Frédéric Hanoteau

Photography Page 1 & 20: Getty Images

Published by Treasure Bay, Inc.
40 Sir Francis Drake Boulevard
San Anselmo, CA 94960 USA

PRINTED IN SINGAPORE

Library of Congress Catalog Card Number: 2008922565

Hardcover ISBN-13: 978-1-60115-203-9
Paperback ISBN-13: 978-1-60115-204-6

Visit us online at:
www.HalfAndHalfBooks.com

A Doctor for the Animals

Table of Contents

Facts: Being a Veterinarian

Julie's New Pet

Story by **Gérard Moncomble**

Illustrated by **Natali Fortier**

Julie

Julie loved animals. She loved dogs and horses and birds. She loved cows and fish and bugs. She also loved her cat named Cactus. (She named him Cactus because sometimes he would stick Julie with his claws.)

Julie liked to hug and pet animals. Sometimes Cactus would let Julie hug him, but most of the time he didn't.

Julie would have liked to hug and pet the dog next door. But he had no time for such things. He was too busy barking.

Julie liked to watch the goldfish in her garden pond. Sometimes she reached into the water and tried to pet them. They would never let her.

The birds wouldn't let her pet them either. As soon as she got near them, they would fly away.

Julie wanted to hug and pet every animal she saw. But she knew that some animals just don't like it very much. So when Julie really needed to cuddle something, she would cuddle her *stuffed* animals. They never barked or scratched or flew away!

One morning, Julie spied a **swallowtail butterfly** in the garden. It was so beautiful! Julie really wanted to pet it. She walked up to it very slowly. She didn't make a sound. Very, very carefully she reached out to touch it. Poof! It flew away!

Julie waved goodbye to the butterfly. Then she pretended that she had wings of her own. She flew among the flowers, flapping her arms like butterfly wings!

All of a sudden, she heard a sound in the bushes. Julie stopped to listen.

Meow! It sounded like a cat. Was it Cactus? Julie looked around and saw Cactus on the grass. It wasn't Cactus in the bushes, so who could it be?

Ruff! Now it sounded like a dog! Was it the dog next door? Julie looked over and saw the dog next door behind his fence. It wasn't him in the bushes, so who could it be?

Ribbit! Ribbit! Now it sounded like a *frog!* Julie's heart began to pound. What kind of strange animal could be hiding in the bushes??

Julie took hold of a branch. She began to pull the branch back, very carefully. Suddenly a loud voice called out to her.

"Hello! How are you?" the voice said.

Julie jumped back, frightened. She wanted to run away and hide! She also wanted to know what was in the bushes. What kind of thing could meow, bark, croak, and talk? Was it a cat-dog? Was it a frog-man? Was it some kind of a monster?

She had to find out.

With one hand, Julie slowly pulled back the branch. And there it was. The monster was a big black bird!

The bird just sat there looking at her. Julie blinked. The bird blinked. Then it opened its beak and said, "Hello! How are you?"

Julie started to laugh. Now she knew where all those sounds had come from. They had come from this **mynah bird**.

Julie knew all about mynah birds. She knew they could **mimic** lots of noises and sounds. They could even sound just like a person.

Julie smiled at the bird and said, "I'm fine, thank you. How are you?"

The bird didn't answer. Julie moved closer. Now she could see that the bird was shaking. Its wing was hanging at its side. The bird was hurt!

Julie wanted to pet the bird, but she could see that it was afraid. She thought it was afraid of her.

Then she saw something moving through the grass.

It was Cactus! He was getting ready to **pounce** on the bird. Julie had to stop him. What could she do?

Julie opened her mouth and let out a loud **roar**—like the mighty roar of a lion. Cactus turned and ran for his life!

Julie smiled proudly. She could mimic the sound of animals, too!

The mynah bird was safe for now, but it needed help. Julie lay down on the grass. In a gentle voice, she said to the bird, "We need to get you to an animal doctor. A **veterinarian** can fix your wing."

Julie reached out and touched the bird. For once an animal did not try to run away from her.

Julie gently lifted the bird. She held it and softly petted its head.

The bird meowed softly. Then it barked. Then it croaked. Finally, it said, "Hello! How are you?"

Julie and her father took the bird to the veterinarian. The vet told them that the bird was someone's pet. It could not live in the wild. It needed a home. Julie's dad said they would try to find the bird's owner. If they couldn't, Julie could keep the bird.

They never did find the owner, so the bird became Julie's pet. The bird liked to be petted. It did not scratch or fly away. It *did* bark and meow from time to time. And Julie liked that just fine!

New Words

Swallowtail butterfly

a type of butterfly with large wings

Mimic

to copy in action or speech

Mynah bird

a black bird with an orange beak that can copy (or "mimic") a human voice as well as other sounds

Roar

the sound a lion makes

Pounce

to make a sudden attack

Animal Doctors

Veterinarians take care of sick animals. They also care for animals that have been in an accident. Vets also care for animals that just need a checkup.

A vet has to gather clues to figure out what is wrong with a sick animal. The animal cannot tell him!

First, the vet has to know what is wrong. Next, he has to find a way to make the animal better.

The vet may give the animal medicine. He may suggest special foods. Sometimes the animal needs an operation.

"Don't worry! He's going to be fine!"

Pet owners love their animals very much. They worry about them. So vets also let pet owners know that their pets will be okay.

People who want to become veterinarians must study and work hard. They must go to college and then to veterinary school. It's not easy!

City Veterinarians

In the waiting room of a veterinary clinic, no two animals are the same!

I LOVE MY DOG.

I TAKE GOOD CARE OF HIM.

Some veterinary clinics stay open 24 hours a day in case of emergencies.

Tuesday Appointments

- 8:00 Mina, parrot
- 8:30 Toothy, rabbit
- 9:00 Tweety, parakeet
- 9:30 Fielding, gray mouse
- 10:00 Rainbow, chameleon
- 10:30 King Kong, ferret

- 2:00 Nibbles, hamster
- 2:30 Triplex, Trio, & Thrice, dog triplets
- 3:30 Genny, puppy
- 4:00 Galapagos, turtle
- 4:30 Livvy, kitten

Sometimes animals have to stay overnight. There are special animal cages for those animals that need to be closely watched.

For the safety of children

VACCINATE your animal!

Vets can give animals shots to protect them from certain diseases. These are called "vaccinations."

23

Country Veterinarians

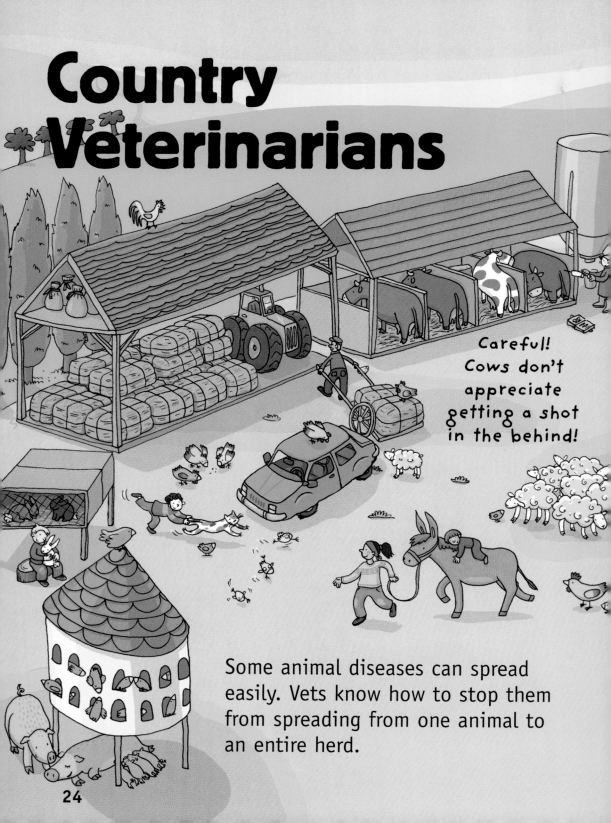

Careful! Cows don't appreciate getting a shot in the behind!

Some animal diseases can spread easily. Vets know how to stop them from spreading from one animal to an entire herd.

A country vet has to leave the office a lot. The animals she works on cannot always come to her. The vet must be ready for any emergency, day or night.

Calves, cows, pigs, sheep, chickens, and rabbits—all these farm animals are taken care of by a country vet.

Some vets devote themselves to animals in the wild. Sometimes, wild animals can be dangerous. It is a good idea for children not to get too close!

 # Veterinarians

Rescue vets try to help wild animals that have gotten into some kind of trouble.

After big oil spills, teams of vets work together to save the lives of birds and other wild animals.

Wild animals are not used to having people around. Often, the vet must shoot the animals with a sleeping drug. Then the vet can check the animal to make sure it is okay.

n the Wild

After rescuing the animal, the vets give first aid.

They wash the birds. They give them food and shots. Once they are well, they let them go back into the wild.

The Leap Frog Race:
A Craft Activity

You will need:

1 sheet of paper
1 pair of scissors
2 yogurt or pudding cups

1 black marker
Scraps of paper
Glue stick

Directions:

1   Copy this upside-down U-shape onto a piece of paper; then cut it out.

2   Turn a yogurt cup upside down, with the opening facing down. Place the straight edge of the pattern level with one side of the yogurt cup and trace its outline. Do this for all four sides.

3   Using your traced lines as a guide, cut out upside-down U shapes out of all four sides of the yogurt cup.

4   Fold the four legs accordion-style as shown.

5   Glue on the pieces of scrap paper to make eyes and a mouth for the frog. Then use the pen to color in where necessary.

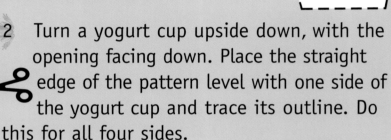

6   Repeat steps 1–5 with the second yogurt cup.

 Race Those Frogs!

To make the frog hop, tap quickly on the top back of its head. It takes some practice. Keep trying!

On your mark! Get set! Go!

The winner is the first frog to reach the end of the track. No pushing!

If you liked **A Doctor for the Animals**,
here is another Half and Half™ book you are sure to enjoy!

It' a Cow's Life

STORY: Grandma is in the hospital and she misses her favorite cow, named Bessie. Nick and his sister decide to bring Bessie to the hospital for a party with Grandma! Do you think the hospital will let a cow in for a birthday party?

FACTS: Did you know that cows don't just eat grass? They swallow the grass, then bring it back up, chew it and swallow it again! You'll learn why cows do this. And you'll learn a lot more surprising things about cows in this fun-packed book.